The
PLANET
ONCE

The Planet Once

iUniverse books may be ordered through booksellers or by contacting:

iUniverse
1663 Liberty Drive
Bloomington, IN 47403
www.iuniverse.com
844-349-9409

ISBN: 978-1-6632-4336-2 (sc)
ISBN: 978-1-6632-4338-6 (hc)
ISBN: 978-1-6632-4337-9 (e)

Library of Congress Control Number: 2022914093

iUniverse rev. date: 10/27/2022

The Planet Once

Jack Branagan

Illustrated by Bob Petillo

The Planet Once was a beautiful planet.

Many forms of life on Planet Once were very similar to those on Planet Earth.

The air, water, and land were pure. The air was cool and clean. The water was crystal blue, and the land was rich with nutrients for plants to grow—until one dreadful day.

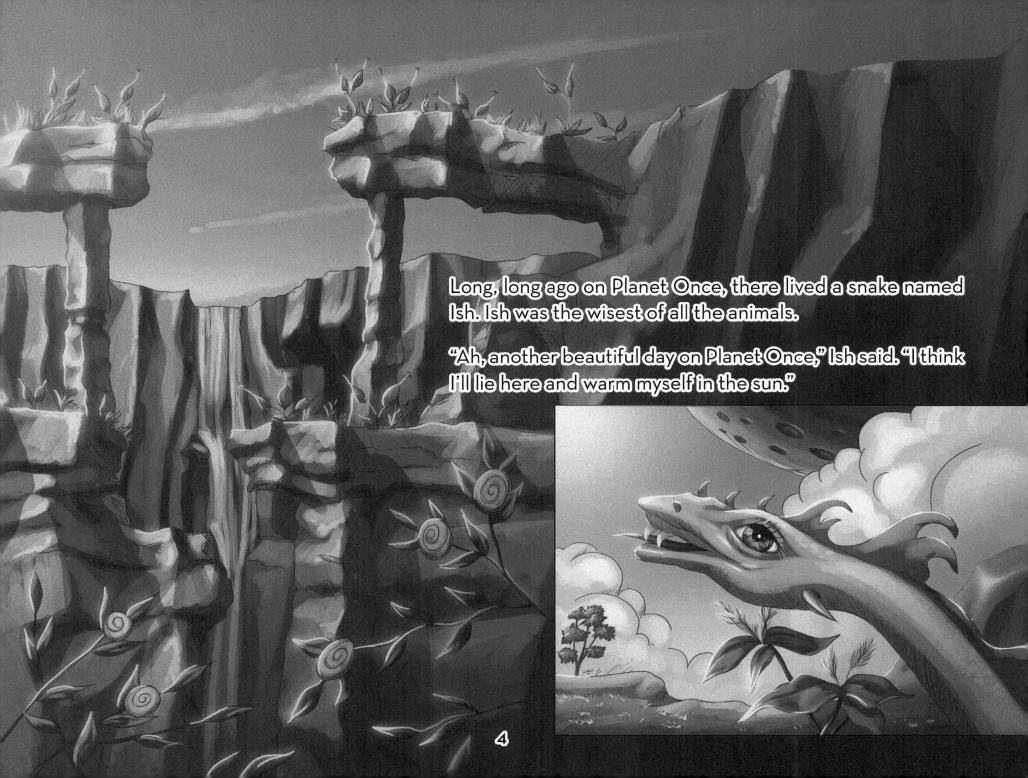

Long, long ago on Planet Once, there lived a snake named Ish. Ish was the wisest of all the animals.

"Ah, another beautiful day on Planet Once," Ish said. "I think I'll lie here and warm myself in the sun."

Just then, Ca flew by, and she stopped to speak with Ish. She was the most colorful of all birds.

"Hello, Ish. What have you been up to lately?" she asked.

"Nothing much," said Ish. "What's new with you?"

Ca flapped her wings, and said, "I've heard some creatures have landed on Planet Once, and they're wasting natural resources."

Ish looked very sad. "Do you mean air, water, and land?"

"Mainly water, but they're also growing some strange-looking things in the soil. I've heard that they are a kind of plant," said Ca.

"Everyone needs to live, Ca. I don't think there will be a problem," answered Ish.

"I'm not sure about that," replied Ca. "I'll tell you what, Ish. I'm going to check this out. I'll be back as soon as I can."

While Ca was gone, Ish went to see their friend Bubble.

Bubble was a mighty big fish. He had a big head, a big brain, and a big mouth to match. "How are you doing, Ish?" asked Bubble.

"I am doing fine, but I am worried," said Ish.

"Worried about what?" asked Bubble.

Ish lowered his head. "Creatures are wasting natural resources."

Bubble looked quite shocked. "All creatures know they must use natural resources wisely. I thought everyone knew about conservation!"

Ish agreed.

"Ish! Bubble! Come quickly!" screeched Ca as she landed on a nearby branch.

"What's the matter, Ca?" asked Ish.

"I learned all about those creatures. They are called *Greedies*. Their leader is called Mr. Greed."

"Do you know what they want?" asked Bubble.

"The Greedies are growing some strange-looking plants in the soil," Ca and Ish told Bubble. "We all need plants for food, places to live, beauty, and even the air we breathe," said Bubble.

"But these plants are different," Ca said.

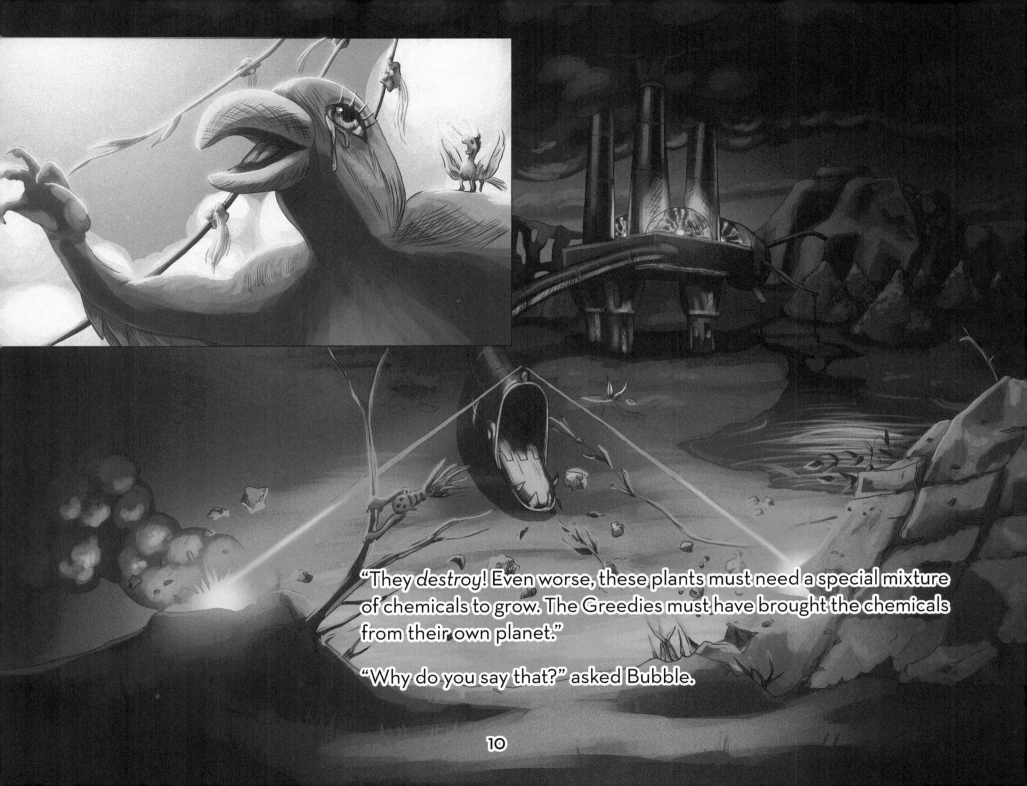

"They *destroy*! Even worse, these plants must need a special mixture of chemicals to grow. The Greedies must have brought the chemicals from their own planet."

"Why do you say that?" asked Bubble.

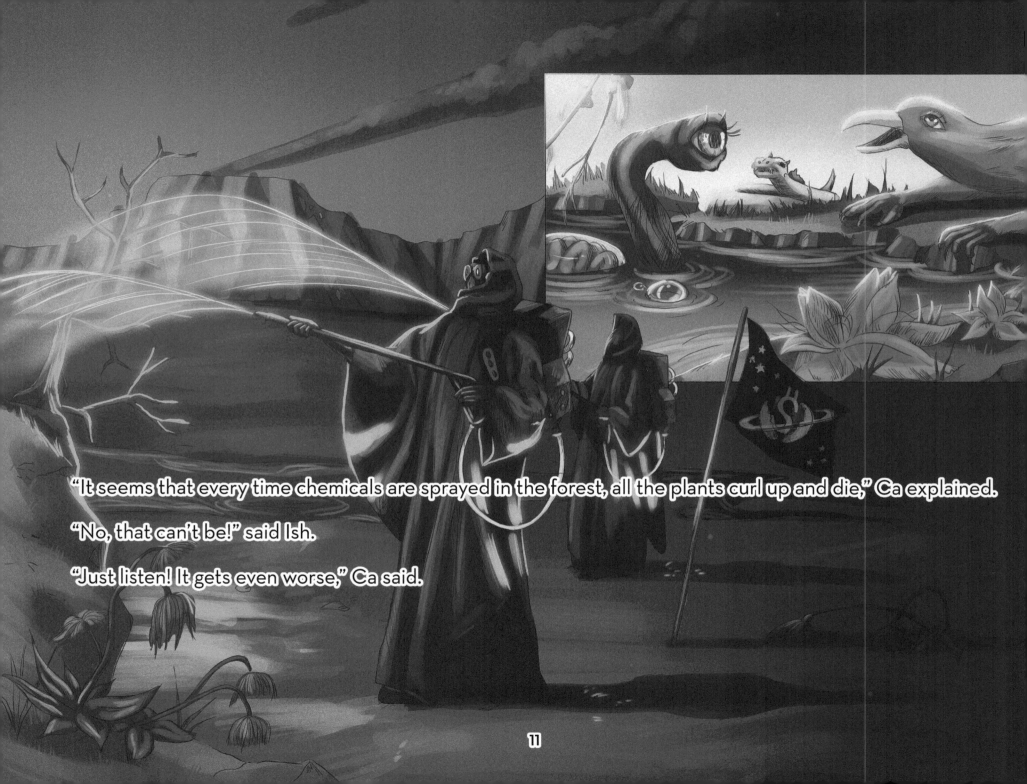

"It seems that every time chemicals are sprayed in the forest, all the plants curl up and die," Ca explained.

"No, that can't be!" said Ish.

"Just listen! It gets even worse," Ca said.

"Since all the plants and trees are gone, every time it rains, the soil is washed into the rivers. The chemicals are getting into the rivers from the soil. The fish cannot live in dirty or polluted water." Ca took a deep breath and wiped a tear from her eye.

"We must stop them!" screamed Bubble.

Ish, Ca, and Bubble set out to meet the Greedies, but Bubble didn't get too far. As he swam downstream, the water became murky. His gills became coated with chemicals. He had a hard time breathing.

Soon, he dropped back to join his friends at the bottom of the river.

Ish and Ca were deeply saddened that Bubble could not continue the journey with them—but they pushed on.

They knew they were getting closer to where the Greedies were working because with every forward motion, fewer and fewer plants and trees could be seen. The rivers were turning a pale shade of red, and the air was thick with smoke and dust.

Ca could no longer see where she was going, so she dropped back as well.

Now, only Ish was left, so he pushed on alone.

Out of the dust and haze, Ish thought he saw a tall tree. As he came closer, he realized it couldn't be a tree, for it had no leaves, and its trunk was very smooth. He thought maybe this was one of the plants Ca had spoken to him about.

Suddenly, Ish heard a loud and angry voice. "Stop! Who goes there?"

Ish was frightened, but he bravely replied, "Ish."

"What do you want?" demanded the voice.

"I represent all of the inhabitants of Planet Once. I must speak with your leader!" Ish exclaimed.

There was a pause. "Wait here!" instructed the voice.

Ish waited a long time.

Then, finally, the leader of the Greedies approached.

14

He had a distrustful look on his face, but he had a friendly voice. "Hello, friend. I am the leader of the Greedies. What can I do for you?" asked Mr. Greed.

"I've come to find out why you are destroying the air, water, and land of Planet Once," Ish said.

"We are just growing some plants to sell back home," said Mr. Greed.

"What do you mean, *sell*? Don't you need them for food, shelter, or medicine?" asked Ish.

Mr. Greed smiled. "Oh no, we're just growing them to make lots and lots of money."

"You mean you don't need these plants to survive?" Ish asked in disbelief.

"I told you. We're just growing them to make money," replied Mr. Greed.

"Sir, if you are growing these things for what you call money, I beg you to stop! You're polluting the air, water, and land and wasting natural resources," Ish said.

"I'm sorry about that. We will be done in a few days, and then we'll leave. Then everything will be fine. I promise."

"If you promise," said Ish.

"Sure. I promise," replied Mr. Greed.

As Mr. Greed turned to walk away, Ish realized that Mr. Greed had two faces—one on the front and one on the back of his head. One was friendly, and the other was wicked.

Yet for some reason, Ish believed Mr. Greed was telling the truth.

Hours turned into days, days turned into weeks, and weeks turned into months. Ish felt that all hope was gone. He realized that Mr. Greed had lied to him. Mr. Greed never intended to leave Planet Once.

Ish decided to return home, but at home, nothing looked the same. Ish cried.

He went to the river, which reminded him of his friend Bubble. Ish thought his imagination was playing tricks on him as he looked into the water. *How can that be?* thought Ish. *Bubble was lost in the muck.* "Bubble? Bubble, is that you?" he asked.

"Yes, it's me," said Bubble.

"Oh, Bubble, I thought you had disappeared."

"I almost did," said Bubble, "but many of my friends and I found clean water at the very bottom of the river."

"We'd better do something now before it's too late!" Ish said. "If only Ca were here to help us."

Just then, Bubble smiled, and said, "She's right behind you."

Ish turned around. "Ca! Ca, I'm so glad you are all right. I thought I never would see you or Bubble again. We must work together and make a plan to rid Planet Once of the Greedies."

Ish, Ca, and Bubble came up with a plan. Ish knew Mr. Greed would not help, but if they could only meet the Greedies—the people who worked for Mr. Greed—maybe *they* would understand.

At that moment, Bubble, with his incredible brain, realized what must be done. He told Ish and Ca about the huge pipes at the bottom of the river. The pipes were like giant vacuums, drawing in everything around them.

"I will swim up one of the large pipes, and then maybe I will get to meet the Greedies!" said Bubble.

Ish was concerned. "Bubble, that might be too dangerous. You don't know what the Greedies might do to you."

"That does not matter," Bubble answered bravely.

If I don't try something, Planet Once will be destroyed.

Bubble swam through the murky water and found the pipe leading to the Greedies' factory. As he swam closer, the current became stronger. He—along with everything around him—was drawn into the pipe.

As he tumbled around and around, Bubble thought he would never live to see another day.

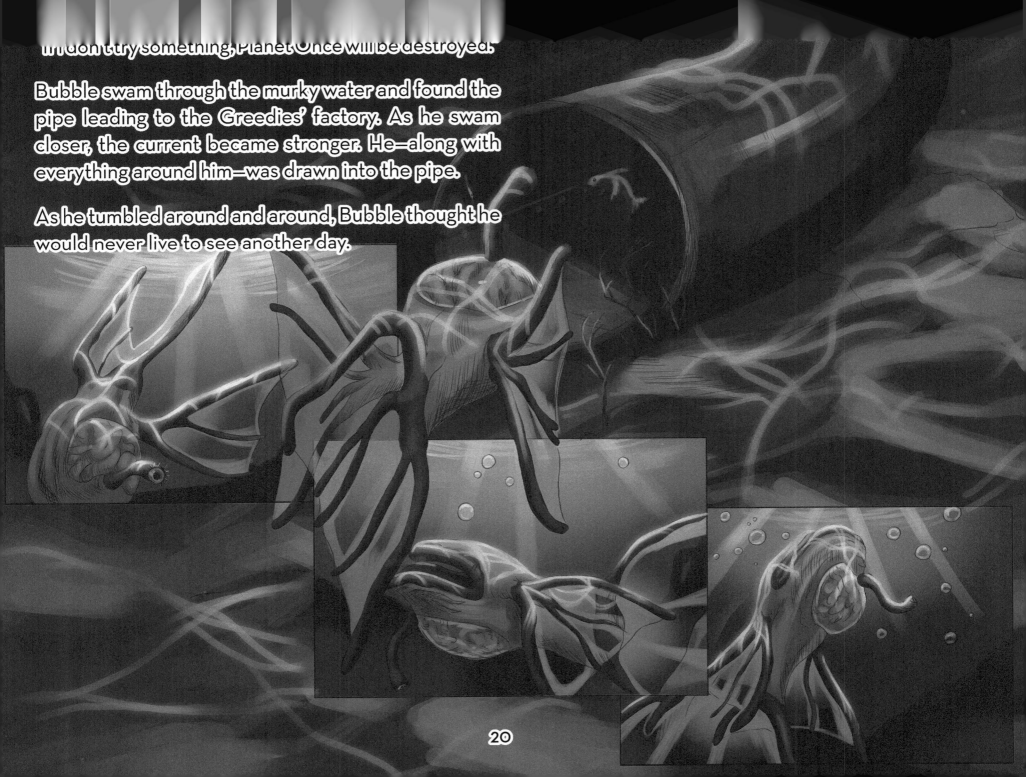

Suddenly, the water calmed down. Bubble found himself in a huge glass tank filled with strange creatures. They all were looking at him.

Outside the tank, the Greedies looked with amazement. They stared at Bubble. They had never seen a form of life such as this.

Suddenly, the brave fish said, "My name is Bubble. I have come to ask you why you are wasting the natural resources and destroying Planet Once."

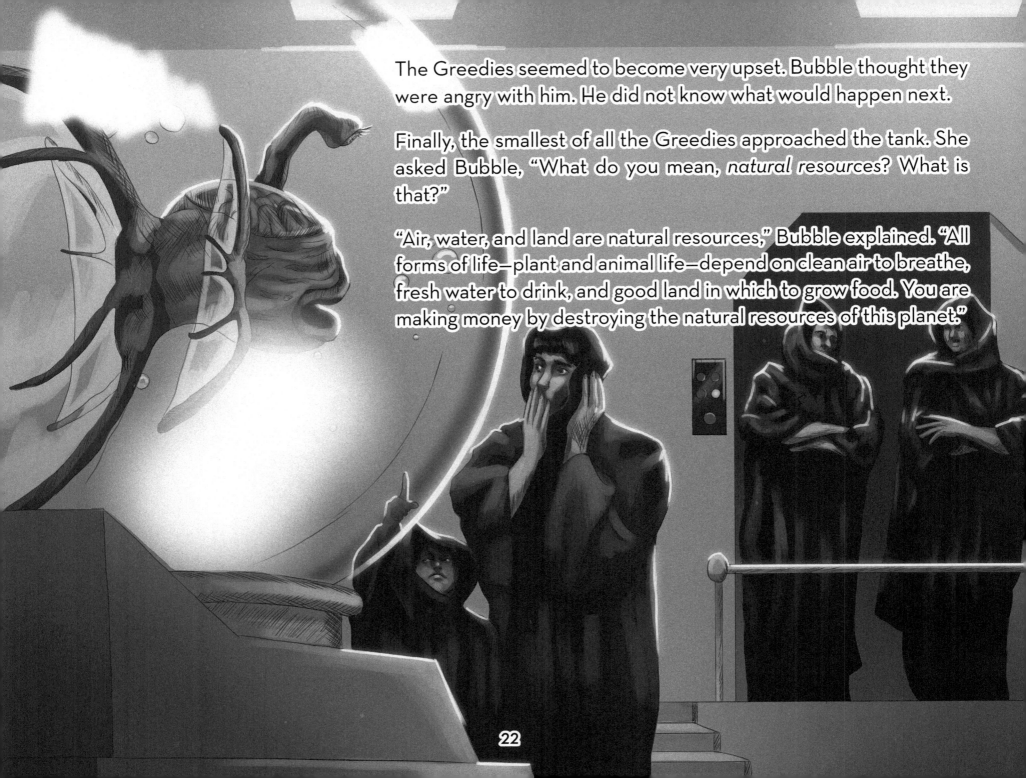

The Greedies seemed to become very upset. Bubble thought they were angry with him. He did not know what would happen next.

Finally, the smallest of all the Greedies approached the tank. She asked Bubble, "What do you mean, *natural resources*? What is that?"

"Air, water, and land are natural resources," Bubble explained. "All forms of life—plant and animal life—depend on clean air to breathe, fresh water to drink, and good land in which to grow food. You are making money by destroying the natural resources of this planet."

The Greedies were shocked. They did not know they were hurting the planet. There were no windows in the factory, except in Mr. Greed's control room. Everyone but the guards worked inside the giant building. The Greedies had no idea what was happening to the planet outside.

Bubble told the Greedies about his friends Ish and Ca and how they were working together to save the planet.

At that moment, Mr. Greed entered the room.

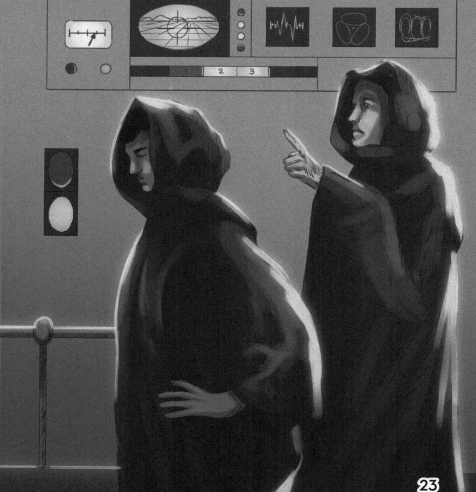

"What's going on here? Why aren't you working? We must make more money!" he growled.

The Greedies became frightened ... but then the smallest of them approached Mr. Greed.

She spoke with a loud, clear voice. "Mr. Greed, why didn't you tell us we were destroying Planet Once and all its natural resources?"

All the Greedies moved closer to Mr. Greed to wait for his answer.

Mr. Greed looked worried. The Greedies had never questioned him before. He turned around and said, "I ... I didn't realize you cared. I, uh, didn't know we were hurting anyone."

Bubble knew Mr. Greed was lying, but he did not say a word.

"Then shouldn't we leave Planet Once as soon as possible and let it heal?" asked the smallest Greedy. "We do not want to destroy anyone's home!"

Mr. Greed thought about what the smallest Greedy had said for a moment and then replied, "Yes! We will go as soon as possible. We will let Planet Once live on."

The Greedies cheered.

A smile came to Bubble's face as he realized Mr. Greed now meant what he said.

The smallest of the Greedies was tossed into the air by her friends. She was the Greedy who first spoke to let Mr. Greed know how everyone felt.

They never realized that if they all worked together to let their leaders know how they felt, things could change.

At that moment, Bubble said, "I will leave at once to tell my friends of your decision. I know they will be very happy." The smallest Greedy reversed the water flow, allowing Bubble to leave the tank. As Bubble turned, he spotted the smallest of all the Greedies.

They looked at each other, and both realized something very special had happened that day.

Planet Once was saved! Just as important, the Greedies learned that it was their responsibility to let their leaders know how they felt.

As Bubble left, the Greedies prepared their giant saucer-like ship to leave. Within a few days, they were packed and ready to go. Even before they left, they could see Planet Once was beginning to heal.

The air was becoming cool and clean.

The water was becoming clear again. Plants were beginning to grow again.

Ish, Ca, Bubble, and Planet Once would survive, but as the friends watched the ship fly off ...

...they wondered where Mr. Greed would take the Greedies next.

CPSIA information can be obtained
at www.ICGtesting.com
Printed in the USA
BVHW061650190123
656627BV00003B/186